EXTRA YARN

BY
MAC BARNETT

ILLUSTRATED BY
JON KLASSEN

SCHOLASTIC INC.

ISBN 978-1-338-27917-7

Text copyright © 2012 by Mac Barnett. Illustrations copyright © 2012 by Jon Klassen. All rights reserved. Published by Scholastic Inc., 557 Broadway, New York, NY 10012, by arrangement with Balzer + Bray, an imprint of HarperCollins Children's Books, a division of HarperCollins Publishers. SCHOLASTIC and associated logos are trademarks and/or registered trademarks of Scholastic Inc.

12 11 10 9 8 7 6 5 4 3 2 1   18 19 20 21 22 23

Printed in the U.S.A.   08

First Scholastic printing, January 2018

Typography by Carla Weise

For Steven Malk
—M.B.

For Mom
—J.K.

On a cold afternoon, in a cold little town,
where everywhere you looked was either the white of snow
or the black of soot from chimneys,
Annabelle found a box filled with yarn of every color.

So she went home and
knit herself a sweater.

And when Annabelle
was done, she had
some extra yarn.

So she knit a sweater for Mars, too.

But there was still extra yarn.

And when Annabelle and Mars went for a walk, Nate pointed and laughed and said, "You two look ridiculous."

"You're just jealous," said Annabelle.

"No, I'm not," said Nate.

But it turned out he was.

And even after she'd made a sweater for Nate
and his dog, and for herself and for Mars,
she still had extra yarn.

At school, Annabelle's classmates could
not stop talking about her sweater.

"Quiet!" shouted Mr. Norman.

"Quiet, everyone! Annabelle, that sweater of yours is a terrible distraction. I cannot teach with everyone turning around to look at you!"

"Then I'll knit one for everyone," Annabelle said, "so they won't have to turn around."

"Impossible!" said Mr. Norman. "You can't."

But it turned out she could. And she did.

Even for Mr. Norman.

And when she was done, Annabelle still had extra yarn.

So she knit sweaters for her mom and dad.

And for Mr. Pendleton

and Mrs. Pendleton. And for Dr. Palmer.

And for little Louis.

She made sweaters for everyone, except
Mr. Crabtree, who never wore sweaters or
even long pants, and who would stand in
his shorts with the snow up to his knees.
"No sweater for me, thanks," said Mr. Crabtree.

So she made Mr. Crabtree a hat.
And even then Annabelle still
had extra yarn.

She made sweaters for all the dogs,

and all the cats,

and for other animals, too.

Soon, people thought, soon Annabelle will run out of yarn.

But it turned out she didn't.

So Annabelle made sweaters for things
that didn't even wear sweaters.

Things began to change
in that little town.

News spread of this remarkable girl who never ran out of yarn.
And people came to visit from around the world, to see all the sweaters
and to shake Annabelle's hand.

One day an archduke, who was very fond of clothes,
sailed across the sea and demanded to see Annabelle.

"Little girl," said the archduke, "I would like to buy that miraculous box of yarn. And I am willing to offer you one million dollars."

"No, thank you," said Annabelle, who was knitting a sweater for a pickup truck.

The archduke's mustache twitched.
"Two million," he said.

Annabelle shook her head.
"No thanks."

"Ten million!" shouted the
archduke. "Take it or leave it!"

"Leave it," said Annabelle.
"I won't sell the yarn."

And she didn't.

So that night the archduke hired three robbers
to break into Annabelle's house,

and they stole the box

and took it to the archduke,
who set off across the snow,
and sailed over the sea,

back to his castle.

The archduke put on his favorite song
and sat in his best chair.
Then he took out the box,
and he lifted its lid, and he looked inside.

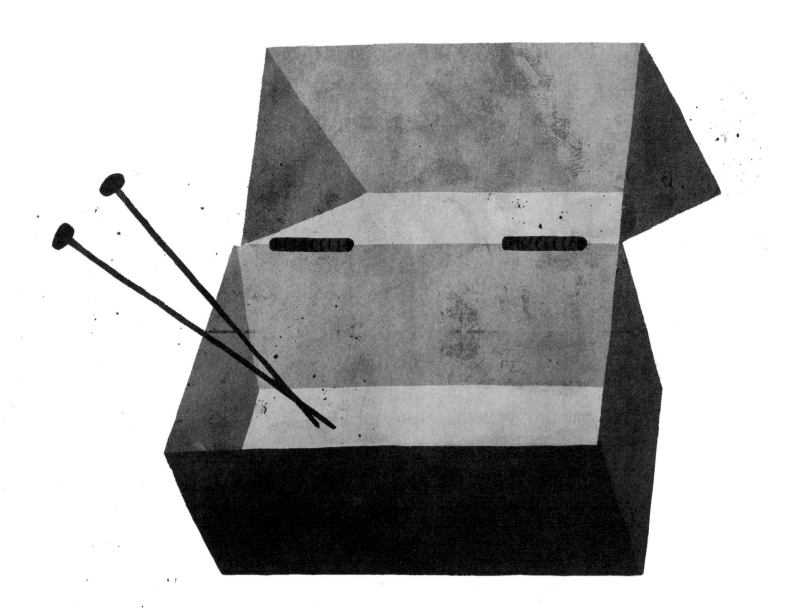

His mustache quivered.

It shivered.

It trembled.

The archduke hurled the box out
the window and shouted,
"Little girl, I curse you with
my family's curse!
You will never be happy again!"

But

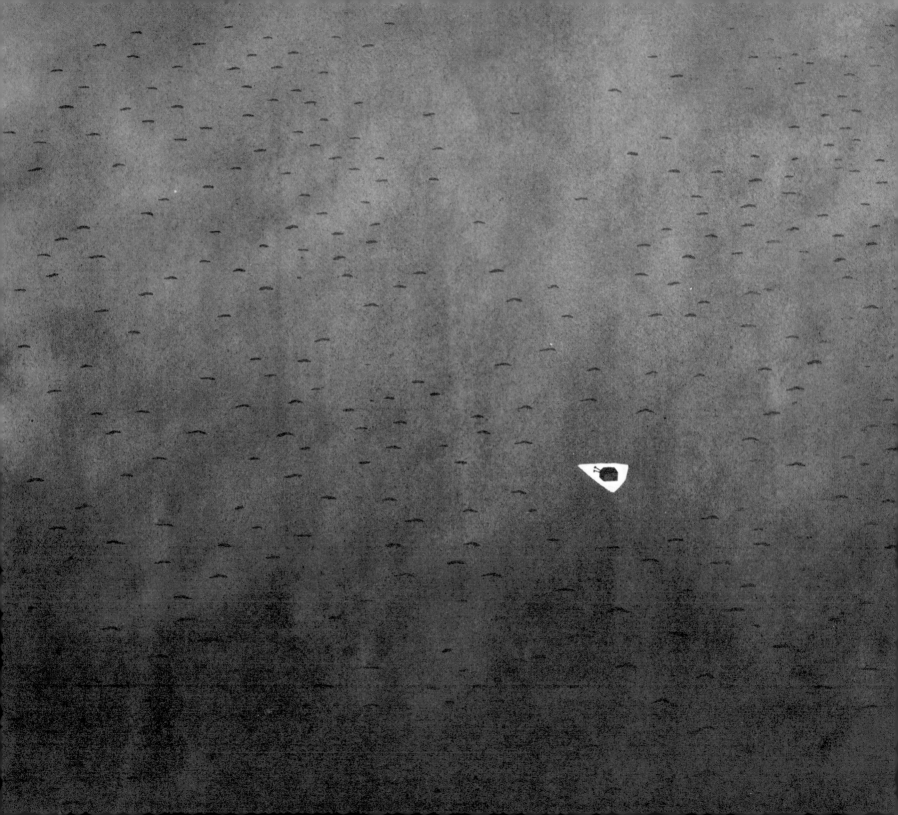

it turned out she was.